CHICKENS! CHICKENS!

A RICHARD JACKSON BOOK

CHICKENS! CHICKENS!

story by BARBARA ANN PORTE
paintings by GREG HENRY

ORCHARD BOOKS   New York

Orchard Books
95 Madison Avenue, New York, NY 10016

Manufactured in the United States of America
Printed by Barton Press, Inc.
Bound by Horowitz/Rae
Book design by Jean Krulis

10 9 8 7 6 5 4 3 2 1

The text of this book is set in 16 point Mixage Medium.
The illustrations are painted with oil-based enamel house paint.

Library of Congress Cataloging-in-Publication Data
Porte, Barbara Ann.
Chickens! chickens! / story by Barbara Ann Porte ; paintings by Greg Henry.
p.   cm   "A Richard Jackson book"—Half t.p.
Summary: A man who loves to draw chickens fortunately meets and marries a woman who not only appreciates his art, but
also finds a way to put it to good use.
ISBN 0-531-06877-3.   ISBN 0-531-08727-1   (lib. bdg.)
[1. Artists—Fiction.   2. Chickens—Fiction.]   I. Henry, Greg, ill.   II. Title.
PZ7.P7995Ch   1995   [E]—dc20   94-19552

There once was a man who drew chickens—chickens, chickens, nothing but chickens.

He drew big chickens and little chickens, fat chickens and thin chickens, red chickens and blue chickens. Sometimes he drew chickens that stood on one leg. He drew chickens in the sunshine and chickens in the rain, chickens on rooftops and chickens pecking grain. That man drew chickens!

"Chickens, chickens, nothing but chickens. Why do you always draw chickens?" the people all said.

"Ah," said the man. "Don't you see? It's because I live on a chicken farm. Everywhere I look, all I see are chickens. Chickens, chickens, nothing but chickens."

Well, he was talking to country people. Everywhere they looked, they saw chickens, too. They didn't need to buy his pictures.

After some time passed, that man moved to the city, seeking his fortune. City sights dazzled his eyes. Now he saw everything. Well, everything *except* chickens. There were no chickens in the city.

Instead, he saw tall office buildings and apartment houses, paved streets and curbed sidewalks, people rushing, trucks and buses, cars and taxicabs, traffic jams at every corner. He saw police walking beats, twirling nightsticks. He saw fire engines and ambulances, though sometimes he only heard their sirens shrieking. He saw dogs chasing cats, and cats chasing mice, and pigeons flying everywhere. Even at night the city was filled with bright lights.

So much commotion, that man thought, and he kept on drawing. But what do you think that man drew now? He still drew chickens—chickens, chickens, nothing but chickens—but you could tell just by looking, these chickens were city birds. He drew chickens on elevators and chickens driving taxicabs. He drew chickens riding school buses, carrying lunch pails and book bags.

"Chickens, chickens, nothing but chickens. Why do you always draw chickens?" the people all said.

"Ah," said the man. "Can't you tell? It's because I love drawing chickens the best. Plus I miss them."

Well, he was talking to city people. What did they know about chickens, except that chickens belonged on a farm? They didn't want to buy his city chicken pictures.

After some more time passed, that man had a bit of good luck. He met a woman who ran a little shop in the city. She sold art and art supplies. They fell in love at first sight.

"I really like your pictures," the woman told the man.

"You do?" said the man. In almost no time they were married. They had children.

The woman gave up her shop. They moved to the farm.

"Country air is so much better for the children," the man told his wife. Also, now that he had a growing family, he had to earn a living sufficient to feed them. Fortunately, except for Sundays, they could do without shoes in the country.

They raised chickens. The woman helped with the work, and collected the eggs, and so did all of the children.

The man still had time to keep on with his drawing. So what do you think that man drew now? He still drew chickens—chickens, chickens, nothing but chickens—but you could tell just by looking, these chickens were pets. They were part of the family. He drew chickens watching babies and babies watching chickens, chickens chasing children and children chasing chickens. He drew one picture of a chicken in the kitchen, sashaying with his wife.

Chickens, chickens, nothing but chickens. What can we do with so many pictures? thought the woman. They were out of storage space entirely. Her own clothes were hanging in the bathroom. Then she had an idea.

First, she carefully arranged the pictures on the wall. Next, she went to work on pillowcases. Well, she had to do something, too, with all those loose chicken feathers and so much down. She traced the man's chicken pictures onto the outsides of the cases and colored them in. She stuffed the cases with feathers and down. Then she made price tags. When she was all finished, she put up a sign:

CHICKENS! CHICKENS!

NOTHING BUT CHICKENS!

PICTURES AND PILLOWS, COUNTRY STYLE.

Finally, she wrote to all her friends and relatives, and also to all her old customers in the city. "Please come. It's a grand opening! I've got a new store."

Everyone came.

"Fantastic!" they said. "Genuine *folk art*." They bought the pictures and pillows and carried them back to the city. They showed them to family and friends. Word spread far and near, and people came from everywhere to buy pictures and pillows, pillows and pictures. The man and the woman grew famous. They got rich. Now they didn't have to sell eggs anymore. They just sold pictures and pillows, pillows and pictures.

Well, they did still keep chickens around.

"For drawing," said the man.

"On account of the feathers and down," said the woman.

Only the children, as they grew up, sometimes complained. "Chickens, chickens, nothing but chickens. It's embarrassing," they said. They meant when friends came to visit, they were always tripping over chickens in the yard.

"Hush," said their mother. "It's been a good living. Haven't they kept you in Sunday shoes all these years? And anyway, your father likes chickens." She herself had never cared *that* much for poultry, but since the day that she first met him, she dearly loved the man. Also, she still admired his drawings.

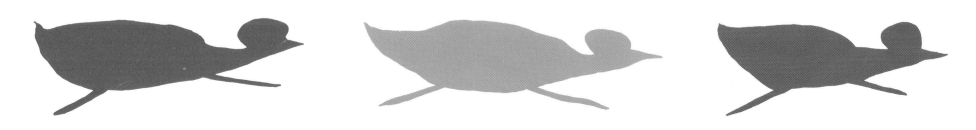

Her husband overheard her speaking to the children. He smiled to himself, and began a new picture. When he was finished, he gave it to his wife. It was a portrait of her, in full color. Not a single chicken was in it. She hung it on the bedroom wall. *It* wasn't for sale.

"I love you," said the man.

"Well of course you do," said the woman. "I love you, too." Then she gave him a quick hug and a kiss and went back to work. When you're running a business, there's always something to do.

Do you want to know how this story ends? The man and the woman lived happily ever after, or at least for a long time to come. So far as I know, so did the chickens. Only the children left home. Sufficiently grown, they moved to the city, seeking their fortunes....